Thaddeus

Thaddeus

Alison Cragin Herzig
and
Jane Lawrence Mali

Illustrated by

Stephen Gammell

LITTLE, BROWN AND COMPANY

BOSTON   TORONTO

TEXT COPYRIGHT © 1984 BY ALISON CRAGIN HERZIG AND JANE LAWRENCE MALI

ILLUSTRATIONS COPYRIGHT © 1984 BY STEPHEN GAMMELL

FIRST EDITION

Library of Congress Cataloging in Publication Data

Herzig, Alison Cragin.
   Thaddeus.

   Summary: Eccentric, fabled Great-Great-Uncle Thaddeus
always makes his namesake's birthday special, but the
seventh celebration is even more wonderful than usual.
   [1. Uncles — Fiction. 2. Birthdays — Fiction]
I. Mali, Jane Lawrence. II. Gammell, Stephen, ill.
III. Title.
PZ7.H432478Th 1984   [E]   84-5725
ISBN 0-316-35899-1

AHS

Published simultaneously in Canada
by Little, Brown & Company (Canada) Limited

PRINTED IN THE UNITED STATES OF AMERICA

For Henry,
twice over

Thaddeus

ON a particular October afternoon, Thaddeus Quimby Jones, also known as Tad, had a birthday party outdoors. He and his friends played Cream the Carrier and ran relay races and followed clues to hidden treasure. Tad's great-great-uncle, Thaddeus Quimby, came dressed as an old man in disguise. He wore a pair of fake glasses with a false nose attached, his long, gray muffler, and his overcoat. Tad had dressed Bear in his circus outfit.

During the lull before lunch, Tad gave out tickets from his ticket booth. Then Tad and all his friends and Bear sat in a circle on the grass to wait for the show. Great-Great-Uncle Thaddeus burst with a flourish from behind a blanket hung between two maple trees and performed stupefying tricks with a dozen raw eggs, some feathers, and a dazed rabbit. The rabbit disappeared twice. The second time, Uncle Thaddeus offered a reward for its return.

After the magic show, Tad perched on a stepladder at the head of a long table decorated with balloons and crepe-paper streamers. Great-Great-Uncle Thaddeus sat in his armchair. He showed Tad and his friends how to catapult stuffed eggs off the end of a spoon. They filled water pistols with lemonade and bombarded each other with sandwich crusts and carrot sticks. For dessert there were ice-cream cones dipped in chocolate sprinkles.

Great-Great-Uncle Thaddeus left the table and went behind the curtain again. When he reappeared he was singing

"Happy Birthday" at the top of his lungs and balancing a three-tiered birthday cake.

On the top tier a chocolate airplane was crash-landed — nose down, tail up — in the middle of a baseball diamond.

On the next layer a circus performer, spangled with edible glitter and filigree trim, hung suspended between a marzipan cannon and a latticed net of icing. A parade of rum-looking camels and plumed carousel ponies propped on drinking straws circled the edge, nose to tail, nose to tail.

On the bottom tier a small band of Indians traveled single file down a rock-candy trail.

Tad jumped off the stepladder. "Where did you get this?" he asked.

"I made it myself," answered his uncle. "At cake school. In the advanced class."

"Even the cannon lady?"

"From scratch," said his uncle. "I baked her head in a ball pan and her body in a wonder mold."

Tad climbed back up his ladder and blew out the seven candles, plus the one to grow on. Then he carefully cut around the decorations and served odd-shaped chunks and wedges of cake to his friends.

When the party was over and all of Tad's friends had finally gone home, Great-Great-Uncle Thaddeus gave Tad a birthday present. The package was the size of a book and it was wrapped in plain, brown paper secured with Scotch tape. Inside the paper *was* a book, but not a book from a store. There were holes punched through the pages along one edge and blue yarn was threaded in and out to hold the pages together. The cover had a lot of writing on it.

"You wrote a book? About me?" asked Tad.

"Every word."

Tad read the title again. "Did you make it up?"

"Not a bit of it," said his uncle. "I wrote it down just as it happened. And illustrated it myself. Here, I'll read it to you."

"I can read it," said Tad. "I'm a good reader. Maybe the best in my class."

"I'm a *very* good reader."

"But it's my book."

"But I wrote it. You can look over my shoulder." Uncle

Thaddeus took off his fake glasses and put on his real ones.

"Okay. I'll turn the pages."

Tad leaned against his uncle and turned to the beginning.
His uncle cleared his throat and began to read.

TAD'S BIRTHDAY BOOK

OR
how against all odds
we solved the
unsolvable problem
and got from there
to this very day

written and illustrated by

Thaddeus Quimby g.g.u.

Chapter 1.

THADDEUS QUIMBY JONES was born on Christmas Day. As soon as his great-great-uncle Thaddeus heard the news, he set off for the hospital to check out his namesake. The weather was foul.

"*Rotten luck,*" *muttered Uncle Thaddeus.* "*A Christmas birthday. Of all the days to be born on . . .*"

There was a wreath decorated with pinecones, red bows, and candy canes on the door of the nursery. A starched nurse wheeled baby Thaddeus in his bassinet to the observation window. She looked as if she smelled brussels sprouts.

Uncle Thaddeus unwound his long, gray muffler and inspected his great-great-nephew. He stared for a long time and then he did a little soft-shoe step, a sort of shuffle-hop-flap-flap to the right and a shuffle-hop-flap-flap to the left.

"*Yes.*" *He nodded and nodded.* "*Yes. You look just like me,*" *he said, extremely pleased.* "*Wrinkled as a winter apple.*"

Baby Thaddeus sneezed.

"*Gesundheit!*" *said his kindly old uncle.* "*I hope they're taking good care of you. I was born in rotten weather, too. The freak snowstorm of*

1883. Over ninety years ago, believe it or not. My father put hot stones in my basket to keep me toasty and he hung a dead spider around my neck to ward off fevers. Worked like a charm."

The nurse came to wheel the bassinet away. Baby Thaddeus screamed until he turned bright red. Uncle Thaddeus rapped smartly on the glass. His eyebrows beetled over his nose. *"No! No!"* he shouted. *"Go change another mewling infant. I haven't given him his birthday present yet!"* He produced a bottle of champagne from one of his coat pockets, removed the gold tinfoil from around the top, and popped the cork. *"Now, where's the cup?"* He patted other pockets. *"Right where I put it."*

He held the silver cup up by its deep, curved handle. It shone in his hand.

"This is even older than I am," he explained. *"Forged by a Thaddeus Quimby to be passed down to a Thaddeus Quimby. It was my baby*

mug and now it is yours. A legacy. My younger brother didn't get one," he added gleefully.

Uncle Thaddeus filled the cup until champagne frothed down the sides and over his fingers. Then he proposed a toast. "Welcome and happy birthday," he said. "Together we'll touch three centuries."

He drained the mug. Baby Thaddeus sucked on his fist. Great-Great-Uncle Thaddeus poured himself another cup and proposed another toast. "To birthdays," he said. "I've had a grand time. We should do this again."

The old cup. A bit worn, but it will still keep your milk cold ---.

"D ID I really scream that loud?" Tad asked. "Did I really turn red?"

"Of course," said his uncle. "This is a true story."

"That's my same cup. The one in my bathroom. I still like it. It's got dents and when I look into it there are two me's."

"You liked everything I gave you," said his uncle.

"What other things did you give me?"

"Turn the page and I'll read on."

Chapter 2.

ONE-YEAR-OLD Tad crawled round and round the Christmas tree. Great-Great-Uncle Thaddeus helped himself to another glass of eggnog. He toasted his nephew. "Life is short but wide," he said. Then he tucked the bowl of ribbon candy under his arm and settled into a chair by the fire to warm his feet.

Little Tad squirmed on his lap. Nice Uncle Thaddeus gave him a sip of eggnog and dangled a gold pocket watch under his nose.

"Mine," said little Thaddeus, grabbing for it. He bit it as if it were a large cookie.

"Clever lad," said his uncle. "Have a good chew. I don't really need it to tell time, you know. I can figure time enough for me by the changing of the seasons and the naming of the moons. The Indians taught me when I as a lad living in Big Hole, Montana. For example, it's winter and you might call this time 'Moon of Strong Cold' or 'Moon When the Snow Drifts into the Teepees.' Or, if there is more ice than snow, you might say 'Moon of Cracking Trees.' And there's always my favorite, 'Moon When the Wolves Run Together.' But if I were in your shoes, I would call it 'Birthday Moon.' Which reminds me. Your pres-

ent." He held out a package. It was the size of a fat business envelope and was wrapped in beautiful yellow paper printed all over with birthday balloons and secured with three rubber bands.

"Mine," said little Thaddeus, letting go of the watch.

"I knew many Indians, mostly Blackfoot, back then," Uncle Thaddeus told him. "When I went tramping in the mountains on the ancient trails, I used to meet them all the time, going the other way."

Little Thaddeus tried to remove the wrapping paper bit by bit from underneath the elastic bands. Uncle Thaddeus tucked the watch back into his watch pocket.

"Let me help you," he said after a while. "I think you've eaten enough paper." He slipped off the three rubber bands and put them around his wrist. "Just what I need," he said, "to keep my socks up when I'm wearing my manure boots."

Rubs Raw and me used to sit up and talk
all night. I think he liked my glasses...

Inside the package was a pair of tiny otter-brown moccasins. They were fringed around the openings and beaded and quilled on the top. The blue and orange and yellow beads glowed in the firelight.

"Here. Give me your feet," said Uncle Thaddeus. He put the moccasins on Tad and tied bows with the thongs that were threaded through the holes in the tongue and side edges. Little Tad's legs stuck straight up in the air. He stared at his feet warily.

"These are ceremonial moccasins," his uncle told him. "The everyday variety are plain. These were made for me on my birthday by the mother of one of my Indian friends."

The watch chimed faintly inside Uncle Thaddeus's pocket. "Today most of my Indian friends in Montana wear wristwatches," he said. "I guess we're all going the same way now." Then he paused. His nostrils quivered. He looked down at his nephew. The toe of one moccasin was darkened with drool and little Tad was contentedly chewing on the toe of the other. Uncle Thaddeus inhaled deeply.

"Ummm. Bacon cooking," he said. "As I remember, moccasins taste as good as they smell."

T.Q.

Moccasins... still good!
Some of the beadwork is
a bit loose, of course...

I KNOW those moccasins!" Tad exclaimed. "The toes are stiff. Mom hangs them on the Christmas tree."

"Everything got hung on the Christmas tree. That was part of the problem."

"It was a big problem," said Tad, "but I didn't realize it at first. I guess I was too little."

"And I was too bird-witted to see that it was only going to get worse."

"I remember one year I knocked over the Christmas tree and all the ornaments got smashed. I think the lights exploded."

"Mercy on us," said his uncle. "Is that what you knocked over? I wrote a slightly different version, as you shall hear."

and there he was, a veritable camel! Well, you can imagine . . . My eyes were out on stalks!

"Later I learned he was a U.S. Army reject, but I didn't know that then. All I knew was that a fabulous animal had dropped from the sky or sprung up overnight like a mushroom in my back lot.

"All day I waited for someone to appear and claim him, and when no one did, I lay awake all night planning. I planned that he would get me out of Big Hole, out of school, away from my brother. Oh, the things I would do with that camel! I would clean him up and he would love me and take me places—to New Orleans, to Brooklyn, to the World's Columbian Exposition in Chicago. Anywhere. Everywhere. Across the river. To adventure."

Tad tugged at the ribbon around his present until he turned red. Then he banged on his uncle's shins. Uncle Thaddeus peered between his knees. His nephew stood up and handed him the box. "Fix it, Go-Go," he demanded.

" 'Adzooks! What happened to my beautiful bows?" asked his uncle. "There's nothing here but knots. I could cut it, but the ribbon's worth saving. Once over with a hot iron and I can use it again." While he attacked the main tangle, he went on with his story.

"I was ready to go before sunrise. The camel was ready too. He was patiently waiting, it seemed, for me to hop on. In my leather pouch I'd already packed all the coins from my bank, my snare, and half a dozen fat rascals—a kind of popover. The only thing left to do was tank him up with fodder and a few buckets of water and we'd be off . . ." Uncle Thaddeus sighed. "It didn't quite turn out that way." He finished untying the blue bows, wound the ribbon around his hand, and pocketed it. He let little Thaddeus have the rubber bands to play with. "No," he said. "It definitely didn't turn out that way."

"The first thing that hit me was his stench. That camel stank to high heaven! But his smell was the least of it. His personality was worse.

"The moment he saw me he set up a howl of protests—long, drawn-out moans and groans of complaint. A real whiner. He kicked and bit at me and only ceased whining long enough to fire off a volley of spittle. And from the other end . . . well, never mind that. I was forced to retreat and reassess the situation. I stared at him and he stared down his flat nose at me through slitted eyes. He looked just like my brother.

" 'Kneel!' I yelled at him. 'Kneel!' Finally I whacked him. I had to. His legs buckled. I didn't pause for thought. I leapt between his mangy humps. He rose, rear end first, while I hung on for dear life. Then he took off. Lickety-split! We lurched right and then we lurched left and we headed toward . . . I'm not sure where. But by then I didn't give a fig! They don't call them 'ships of the desert' for nothing. I was pea-green seasick!

At that point I abandoned adventure. I decided to dismount, but the beast was picking up speed."

Tad had a faraway look in his eyes and rubber bands hanging out of his mouth. He chewed and listened to them squeak.

"That camel thundered down Main Street," Uncle Thaddeus went on, "past the general store and the livery. The saloon was my last chance. As its sign passed over my head, I seized upon it and was left dangling from a wooden bottle high above the ground. I swung there, creaking, and watched that despicable animal hightail it into the rising sun with his nose in the air." Great-Great-Uncle Thaddeus paused. "They got me down," he said, "but only finally."

Little Thaddeus had removed the yellow birthday paper and was prying at the lid of the box. He was still chewing on the rubber bands. His uncle took them back, dried them on his vest, and slipped them onto his wrist. "Just what I need," he said, "for when I reglue the handle of my stove broom."

"What's this?" asked Tad, peering into the open box.

"What's what? Oh, that's your present," said Uncle Thaddeus. "My old baseball bank. The very one I took my pennies out of to finance my adventure."

His nephew held up a leather drawstring pouch.

"Pennies. Brand-new ones. Just for you. Here. I'll show you how the contraption works."

The pitcher wore a white uniform with black lettering. There was still some red paint on his hat. Uncle Thaddeus put a penny in the pitcher's hand and pressed a lever. The pitcher threw the penny to a batter, the batter swung and missed, and the penny disappeared through a slot in the catcher's mitt.

"Push it," said smart little Tad.

His wonderful uncle showed him how to press

the lever and together they banked all the rest of
the pennies. The batter always missed, but the
catcher never did. When the pennies were gone,
Thaddeus showed his nephew how to open the
bottom of the bank so the pitcher could pitch
them again.

Then the old geezer had himself a snooze.
When he woke up, Tad was playing with the bank
by himself. "Mine," he said.

I STILL play with that bank," said Tad. "You gave me my best birthday presents."

"It wasn't hard," said his uncle. "I didn't have much competition."

"What did you give me for Christmas?"

"Nothing. Everyone else took care of that."

"Did you ever think of giving me a camel?" Tad asked.

"Yes, but I figured I could never slip it by your parents. So I came up with another idea."

"What was it?" Tad asked.

Uncle Thaddeus smiled and read on.

Chapter 4

"WHERE'S my birthday present?" asked Tad on the next Christmas afternoon.

"It's in the right-hand pocket of my coat," said Great-Great-Uncle Thaddeus. He whisked the snow off a tree stump with the fringe of his gray muffler and sat down.

Tad reached into the pocket up to his elbow.

"Slowly, slowly," cautioned his uncle. "He may be dozing and he's shy with strangers."

Slowly, slowly, Tad pulled out his present. The present was unwrapped. It was a small stuffed bear made of brown plush. He had black button eyes and his ears, the size of gingersnaps, stood up alertly. His arms and legs were movable.

"He's awake," said Tad.

"I suspect he was sleeping with one eye open because he was looking forward to meeting you," said his uncle. "Bear, this is my namesake, another Thaddeus Quimby. He is three years old today and he doesn't like olives. Tad, this is Bear. Bear is seventy-four years old and he's in tip-top condition. Not an ounce of flab on him. I found him in Morris Michtom's candy store in Brooklyn. I remember the year exactly. It was 1902. Mr. Michtom told me he had stayed up half the night cutting out a pattern, sewing it together, and

stuffing it. Mrs. Michtom was just putting Bear in the window when I happened by. A look passed between us. There was nothing for it but to buy him. He's the first stuffed bear, give or take a bear, ever made. The George Washington of bears, you might say."

Tad lifted Bear up until they were nose to nose. "He likes me," he said.

"His given name is Teddy's Bear," said his uncle, "after Teddy Roosevelt, a famous American president who loved battles and children and food and baby bears. But I've always called him Bear."

"He wants to see my bed," said little Tad.

"Of course he does," said his great-great-uncle.

Inside the house Tad put his small galoshes next to his uncle's big ones and climbed the stairs with Bear.

A bit later he came down and reported, "Bear says, 'Okay.' He wants to stay."

T.Q.

U.S. ARMY

Never saw Teddy with any big stick,
But he carried that bear all over! I drew
this from an old photo i took.

The old man looked up from his chair by the fire. "That's settled then," he said and slapped his knee. "He'll need his things." He handed little Tad a package the size of a cigar box. It was wrapped in creased yellow paper printed all over with birthday balloons and held together with several rubber bands.

"I'll take those back, thank you very much," said his uncle, looping the rubber bands around his wrist. "Just what I need to keep my cupboard doors from drifting open whenever they feel like it."

Tad opened the box. Inside there was something long and skinny and gray.

"Bear's muffler. I knit it myself," said Uncle Thaddeus proudly. "My brother's wife, your great-grandmother, taught me how."

"What's this thing?" asked Tad, holding up a tiny, turquoise tank-suit shot through with silver threads and embroidered with sequins.

"His circus outfit," his uncle told him. "Hermione made it for him. Every teensy stitch. When she was in the hospital. I've told you about Hermione. Remember?"

"No," said Tad.

"Miss Hermione Zazell!" intoned his uncle. "Well, she was a most remarkable lady. I loved her. Better than anyone I ever knew—until you, that is. She was more dazzling than a shooting star, faster than a hummingbird. That's how she flew. I only saw her fly once, but once was enough for a lifetime."

"Like Superman?" asked Tad.

"Heaven's, no! She was a human cannonball!" said his uncle. "A circus star. Shot from a cannon twice a day. The one time I saw her perform was a night full of unexpected disasters." He clasped his hands and sighed. "A hurricane blew up out of nowhere just as the circus began. The rain poured down and the wind whipped under the tent. A tree blew over and crushed the generator

—all the lights went out, so they had to use pine-knot torches and candles instead. I remember the smoke stung my eyes. Then lightning struck the center pole. The crowd screamed. Someone threw a rock at the bassoonist. Just at that moment they fired off Hermione. She burst out in a thunderous billow of smoke and soared over my head. She was wonderful!" He clapped his hands together. "Wonderful!"

Tad clapped, too, and stared up at his uncle.

"But she missed the net," Great-Great-Uncle Thaddeus went on. "She was carried out on a stretcher. That's how I met her—in the hospital, just the way I met you. I showered her with champagne and flowers and candy. I gave her Bear for company. We had six perfect weeks together, or so I thought. Then her legs healed and she ran off with the man who could balance on fourteen chairs. All that was left in her hospital bed was Bear in his circus suit."

Uncle Thaddeus stared into the fire. Tad held
up Bear and the circus suit. "Dress him, Uncle
Go-Go," he said.

T.Q.

BEST friend I ever had!
(besides you, Tad)

GREAT-GREAT-UNCLE THADDEUS stopped reading. He took a large handkerchief out of his pocket, mopped his eyes, polished his glasses, and blew his nose.

"Do you still remember her?" asked Tad.

"Indeed I do. Every hair on her head." He stuffed the handkerchief back into his pocket.

Tad picked up Bear and threw him as far as he could. "Bear remembers her too," he said. Then he picked Bear off the grass and tossed him again. Bear somersaulted through the air. "Look! Bear's in the circus," he shouted. "But . . . I've never even seen a circus."

"I can fix that, by Jove," said Great-Great-Uncle Thaddeus. "Next year on your birthday. We can go early and stay late. The sky's the limit. We can do anything we want on your birthday now."

"And we couldn't before," said Tad. "It used to make me sad and I always spit up the plum pudding. But it doesn't say that in the book. Is there more about me in the next chapter?"

Uncle Thaddeus rifled through a few pages.

"Aha!" he said and began to read.

Chapter 5

AT Christmas dinner a year later, Great-Great-Uncle Thaddeus sat at one end of the long table. His great-great-nephew sat next to him with Bear. Bear wore an astronaut suit made of aluminum foil, and his knitted, gray muffler.

Dessert was plum pudding on a platter decorated

Always wait a few minutes before dessert. Let the vegetables settle . . .

all around with sprigs of holly. Someone had stuck four birthday candles in the pudding, one for each year. Tad blew out the candles and put them into his pocket. He smelled his helping of plum pudding and gave it to Bear. Bear turned up his nose.

"It looks positively disgusting, I know," said Uncle Thaddeus, "but it's not half bad. Pass it here."

"Real birthday cakes have icing," said his nephew. "Lots and lots of icing. I know. I went to a real birthday party once. An outer-space party, with games and balloons and prizes and a cake with rockets on it. I never had a cake like that. I never had a cake."

"Well, when I was young there were lots of things I didn't have," said his uncle. "For instance, talking movies and television. There were no electric stoves, no electric toothbrushes, no electric blankets. I wore heavy woolly underwear, which gave me itches. We didn't have vacuum cleaners, refrigerators, washing machines, air conditioners. There weren't any."

"Why not?" asked Tad.

"Nobody had invented them yet."

"Did you have a bed? Did you have a mother?"

"Indeed I did, but I never had a great-great-uncle."

"Still?" asked Tad.

"Still," answered his great-great-uncle.

"Did you have a birthday cake?"

"Yes. But I didn't have pepperoni pizza."

"Did you have birthday presents?" asked Tad.

"Is that a hint?" asked his uncle. "Thought you'd catch an old buzzard asleep, did you? Go rummage through my coat pockets."

Uncle Thaddeus was sipping his after-dinner coffee by the fire when Tad reappeared carrying a package the size of a rolled-up magazine.

The present was wrapped in wrinkled yellow paper printed all over with birthday balloons and secured at each end with thick rubber bands. Tad handed the rubber bands to his uncle.

"Just what I need," said Thaddeus, "to replace the missing spring of my gas pedal."

The paper unrolled. Some green goggles and a worn brown thing with a dangling strap fell out onto Uncle Thaddeus's lap.

"I can tell by your face," said Uncle Thaddeus after a moment, "that you wish you could hide this stuff under a chair. But don't be too hasty. When I put them on, you'll know exactly what they are."

Thaddeus fitted the brown thing on his head, snapped the strap under his chin, and adjusted the goggles over his eyes.

"Now, what do you see?" he asked.

"A frog?" guessed Tad. "In a funny hat?"

"No, no, no, you mousemeat!" said his uncle.

Just about to take her up...
always carried my lunch though.
A plum a day, i always say...

T.Q.

"What you see is a young, reckless, resourceful, daredevil pilot." He threw back his shoulders and stuck out his chest. "One of the first American aviators, looking for glory. Our planes were as fragile as cereal boxes—only cloth and wood and wire held together by glue. And tricky to fly. They'd just as soon crash as get off the ground. Who cared? Not us. All we wanted was excitement. Imagine a frigid, predawn morning. I slip my flying suit on over my pajamas, slide my feet into sheepskin moccasins, and reach for these very goggles and this very helmet. And my—"

"Over your jammies? That you slept in?" asked Tad. "You went in an airplane in your pajamas?"

"Certainly. They were warm and cozy and my underwear was cold and limp. And now for my muffler . . ." Uncle Thaddeus peered around. "I need my muffler. Run, quick, and get it, there's a good lad," he said to Tad. "It's in the umbrella stand."

Tad came running back with the muffler and Uncle Thaddeus wrapped it twice around his neck and let the ends dangle. He took a last swig of coffee. "Now, I'll take you on a training flight.

Here's my plane." He patted an imaginary fuselage. "Thoroughly unreliable and constantly in need of repair. Put her into a steep dive and pray the wings don't drop off. Never mind."

"The cockpit"—the old pilot closed his eyes and sniffed—"smells of gasoline and castor oil. I lock my seat belt, click. Signal to my mechanic. 'Switch off!' I yell at him. 'Suck in! . . . Contact!' The mechanic snaps down on the end of the propeller and my machine roars to life—brrm brrm—in a blue-gray cloud of smoke. Open the throttle and keep the stick . . . the stick?" Uncle Thaddeus snatched up the fireplace shovel and held it between his legs. "And keep the stick well forward. We're picking up speed, bump, bump, bump over the grass. The tail lifts, ease the stick back." Old Thaddeus stood up and began to jog. He jogged out into the hall. Tad ran after him.

"We're up and away. Thirty feet, forty feet,

cleared the fence. Cleared those trees. Just missed the church steeple. That's always dicey."

Great-Great-Uncle Thaddeus hunched over his shovel and swiveled his head from side to side, scanning the sky.

"Blizzard," he announced grimly. "This could be unpleasant. Too late to land. Have to take it head-on. Hang on, my boy," he said to little Tad right behind him. "Can't see my instrument board. Windshield fogged."

Uncle Thaddeus looked over the edge. "Still can't see. Ow! Snow feels like needles at sixty miles an hour." He wiped off his goggles and then the windshield with one end of his muffler. "We could be flying upside down for all we know." Uncle Thaddeus lurched back into the living room bent sideways like a rhinoceros with a stiff neck. He careened around the Christmas tree at a steep tilt.

"*Blast and tarnation! One of my field boots just fell out and there goes the bag of bombs. Hope the blessed wings don't buckle. Got to get out of this soup. There's a cow pasture. My stars. What a godsend.*" He circled the carpet twice. "*Oh, no! What a catastrophe! It's riddled with humps and bunkers and hazards, but we have no choice. If we can just clear . . . look sharp, my boy— uh oh, uh oh—thwam-thwack-snapple-CRASH!*" The courageous pilot dropped the shovel and flung his arms over his face. Then he doubled over and peered between his legs at his nephew. "*Had to bird's-nest,*" he said. "*In this blue spruce. That's what we called it when we landed in a tree. Not to worry. A farmer will be along shortly to get us down. Quite an adventure, don't you think?*"

Little Tad nodded through his legs at his uncle. Then he tucked Bear into the back of his corduroy pants. "*My turn to be pilot,*" he said.

Always fit sort of
tight. Used to get bad
headaches now and then...

T.Q.

WHAT if the tree hadn't been there?" asked Tad. "We would have used our parachutes, right?"

"Wrong, wrong, wrong! No pilot worth his salt would have been caught dead with one of those namby-pamby bedsheets. We left them in our lockers."

"That's dumb."

"Perhaps. But at the time it was the only way to go."

The breeze ruffled the pages of the book.

"Did you do any other dumb things?" asked Tad hopefully.

Great-Great-Uncle Thaddeus smiled and picked up the book again.

Chapter 6

*L*ATE in the afternoon on the following Christmas, Great-Great-Uncle Thaddeus shuffled rapidly up the walk. One end of his gray muffler brushed the ground. His nephew, wearing his leather helmet and goggles, flew out of the house to greet his favorite relative.

"I've been waiting and waiting!" said Tad. He danced around his uncle and tugged on his muffler. "My birthday present's been here all day. Hurry up, Uncle Go-Go! Where have you been?"

"Slow down, old boy," said the doddering relict. "I'm not quite myself. A little rocky on my pins. Lend me your shoulder up these steps."

"I saved you a whole plateful of stuff," little Tad told him. "Turkey and sweet potatoes and gravy and nuts and candy . . ." The sleigh bells on the front door jangled.

"Aaaggh," groaned Tad's uncle, making for his chair by the fire.

"You still have your coat on."

"I can only do one thing at a time today," said Great-Great-Uncle Thaddeus, "and right now I'm sitting." He loosened his tie. Then he unbuttoned his vest. And then he let out his belt. "Ahh," he sighed. "That's better."

"I can bring you your plate right here," offered

his nephew, "and I'll open my present while you eat."

"No food," said his uncle, "ever, ever again. I've already eaten. A whole cake and a pan of ice cream. Not to mention the icing, which was separate."

Well, i had all the right ingredients for my cake... still don't know what went wrong —

"I love icing," said his nephew. "Why didn't you bring me some?"

"I tried, believe me, I tried. In fact, that was the whole idea," said his uncle. "A birthday party with all the trimmings. 'A little cake, a little ice cream. What could be easier?' I said to myself this morning. 'I'll whip it up in no time and surprise the birthday boy.' "

"A cake, a whole cake? And ice cream? And candles, all for me? Where is it? Where is it?"

"It's a long story." Uncle Thaddeus rubbed his stomach. "But without dwelling on it, I can tell you that one square of semisweet chocolate and fifteen marshmallows won't turn into ice cream no matter what you add. I drank that. As for the cake, I thought I could glue the bits and crumbs together with icing, but it all balled up on the end of the knife. I've eaten enough cake balls to last me for a lifetime." His stomach burbled.

Tad watched him anxiously.

*"What a pity! But it's the thought that counts,"
his uncle said. "Be a good fellow and get me a
glass of soda water. With a twist of lemon." Then
he belched. "Never mind," he said. "I think
everything just hit bottom." He burped again and
rebuckled his belt.*

*"Can we at least do my present now, Uncle
Go-Go? That's it, isn't it? Over there? By the
Christmas tree?"*

*The present was the size of a refrigerator. It
was draped in an old bedsheet. The sheet was
decorated all over with real balloons and tied
securely at the bottom with pale blue ribbon.*

*"That's part of it," said Great-Great-Uncle
Thaddeus. "The second part. The first part is in
my pocket."*

*The package was the size of a tie box. It was
wrapped in tattered yellow paper printed all over
with birthday balloons and held together with a
rubber band.*

Tad handed the rubber band to his uncle.

"Forget about saving the paper this year," said Uncle Thaddeus. "It got scorched last time I ironed it."

Tad held up a slat of varnished wood with letters carved and painted on it. "What does it say?"

"OPEN," read his uncle. "Nice word. I wish it were still open."

"Open? What was open?"

"The restaurant that I rejuvenated, renovated, recycled, and restored from a merry-go-round," explained Uncle Thaddeus. "The Carousel Restaurant. The fastest revolving restaurant ever. The only restaurant where you ate in the saddle, going up and down, round and round.

"Waiters circulated with mustard and emergency soup and seconds. Macaroon jam tarts, blueberry betty, roundabout doughnuts and sunshine cake," said old Thaddeus. "Popcorn balls," he added, "and ice-cream banana boats. Children loved it."

"Did they have birthday parties there?" asked Tad.

"Dozens of them," answered his uncle. "You had to book in advance. The waiters sang 'Happy Birthday' and the children hung on to the poles and ate one-handed. Many rode double. The daring ones didn't hold on at all. Others wouldn't let go and had to be pried loose by their parents. Adults were admitted only when accompanied by a child."

Uncle Thaddeus paused and pulled on the hairs sprouting out of his ears. "That was a big mistake. One of the dumbest things I ever did. Should have kept them out entirely. They hadn't the stomach for it.

"Mothers came over queer and threw up in the dragon chariots and the whale cars. Fathers complained about spots on their ties.

I remember that our
Root Beer Floats were always
a problem . . .

"Finally we had to close." Old Thaddeus turned the sign over. "CLOSED," he read. "I like OPEN better. Go ahead. Open the other part."

Under the sheet was a six-sided wooden structure. It had a door with a brass key, and a window with a metal grille and a green pull-shade. Tad discovered that the shade really worked.

"This was the restaurant ticket booth, but it could be anything," his uncle told him.

Under the window were two hooks. He showed Tad how to hang the sign on the hooks. Tad hung it OPEN-side out, unlocked the door, and went in. He went in and out many times, stowing things. Finally he went in, closed the door, and didn't come out again.

"I need Bear," he called to his uncle through the window.

His uncle squeezed Bear under the grille.

"Make the sign say CLOSED," Tad said. Then he pulled down the shade.

CLOSED

T.Q.

Always had fun in the
ticket booth... you can have
fun just about ANYWHERE, you know!

A while later, through the walls of the booth, Uncle Thaddeus heard singing. He did not join in, because he was eating a banana. After a few bites he decided that the banana was too green. So he reclosed the peels and fastened them securely with the rubber band from around his wrist. Then he put the banana in his pocket for tomorrow, but all the time he listened to Tad sing. The voice sounded muffled and sad:

"Happy birthday to me . . . Happy birthday to me . . ."

TAD looked over at the ticket booth. "I *was* sad, I remember," he said.

"Yes," said his uncle. "You were sad and so was I. And that's when I resolved to do something about it."

"And you did! I remember. I remember exactly how it happened. Is it in the book?"

Great-Great-Uncle Thaddeus nodded.

"*All of it?* Let me read."

"Later." His uncle held on to the book. "I'm almost through."

Chapter 7.

*T*HE next Christmas the snow was wet and heavy. Perfect for snowballs. Great-Great-Uncle Thaddeus tucked his trousers into his old, black galoshes and put a rubber band around the top of the one with the broken buckle.

Outside, he scooped up a mittenful of snow

and demonstrated for Tad how to pack and turn, pack and turn, until it became a hard, round snowball. Then he rocked back on his heels, took dead aim at the red flag on the mailbox, and hurled. The snowball sailed past the mailbox and exploded in the bird feeder, terrifying a gray squirrel.

"He won't come nosing around anymore," said Uncle Thaddeus.

Tad's snowball stuck from one mitten to the other.

"I'll make the arsenal," said his uncle, "and you fire them off."

Tad threw a snowball at the front door and hit the wreath. Uncle Thaddeus packed as fast as he could.

"I can't keep up with you," he said.

"I'm six, you know," said Tad.

"I'm ninety-six," said his uncle, "and I'm pooped."

"Maybe you're hungry," suggested his terrific nephew.

There was a gingerbread house on the counter in the kitchen. After shedding his coat and gray muffler, Uncle Thaddeus made a beeline for it. He ate a shutter off one of the side windows, where he figured it wouldn't show. Then he ate a gumdrop bush.

T.Q.

Always liked shutters...
these were lemon!

"Uncle Go-Go! Where's my birthday present? There's nothing in your coat pockets. I've looked and looked."

His uncle's mouth was full. He was eating the gingerbread chimney. It was bigger than he'd thought.

"It's going to be delivered? Like last year?" asked his nephew.

Uncle Thaddeus shook his head and made a face. He had discovered that the spun-sugar smoke was really cotton.

"Are we going to go get it?" asked Tad.

Uncle Thaddeus shook his head again.

"You forgot! I'll bet you forgot! Everybody forgets it's my birthday, too!" Tad kicked the refrigerator. "Dumb plum pudding! Dumb Christmas!"

Uncle Thaddeus finally got the chimney down.

"Forget? Me forget! What a dastardly sugges-tion. Forgetting has never been one of my problems. I have a memory like nothing. Of course I have a present. It's just that it's a different kind of present. The kind that can't be wrapped."

"Why? Is it so big? Bigger than my ticket booth?"

"I don't know how big it is," his uncle said. "It's more an idea than a thing. It's a day."

"What do you mean?" asked Tad suspiciously.

"A new birthday," explained his uncle. "The birthday you've got is too crowded. There's no room for you. So I thought I'd give you mine."

"Can you do that?" asked Tad. "Are you allowed?"

"Certainly! If you happen to be a special person and another special person wants to give you his."

"Are you sure it will work?"

"Absolutely! We can make anything work if we put our heads together."

After a moment Tad asked, "Don't you want it anymore?"

"I hardly use it," answered his uncle, "and it's

too good a day to waste. It's full of happy memories."

"When is it?" asked Tad.

"It's not over New Year, or anywhere close to the Fourth of July or Thanksgiving. And it's not stuck off in August when nobody's around. It's perfect: It's October tenth. Right in the middle of Indian summer."

"Can my friends from school come?" Tad asked.

"Absolutely. All of them. Hundreds!" exclaimed his uncle. "Is it a deal?"

"Deal!" said Tad.

They shook hands.

"Done!" said the crafty old uncle.

"Will I get a birthday present then?" asked Tad.

"Indeed yes!" his great-great-uncle assured him. "I'm working on it already. In fact, I've been working on it for a long, long time."

GREAT-GREAT-UNCLE THADDEUS closed the book and presented it to Tad. Tad held it in both hands.

"This is it, isn't it? The thing you've been working on for a long, long time?"

His uncle nodded.

"I liked the part about me being a baby best. And I remember it, I think. I did such funny things." Tad turned the pages. "Is there any more?"

"More! This took me a lifetime!"

Tad stood up and handed the book to his uncle. "I have to go get something," he said. "Keep this for me. I'm going to read it to Bear tonight."

A few minutes later Tad came back with a box. It was the size of a birdhouse.

"What's this?" asked his uncle.

"A birthday present. For you."

Uncle Thaddeus undid the string. The lid popped off and rubber bands of every size, sort, and color spilled out onto the table. "Hot spit!" he said, diving into the box with both hands. "How did you know I'd run out?"

"I bought five pounds," explained Tad. "I hope it's enough. Six hundred thousand million, about."

His uncle slipped some rubber bands onto his wrists and some into each of his pockets. Then he and Tad shared a candy camel and Tad poured the last of the lemonade into two paper cups. Uncle Thaddeus proposed a toast.

"To birthdays," he said.

"And more cakes," said Tad. "And more presents."

The rabbit nosed out from under the tablecloth and scuttered into the ticket booth. Tad picked up Bear, gathered up a fistful of leftover carrot sticks, and went in after him.

Uncle Thaddeus dozed in the late afternoon sun. A red-and-yellow leaf drifted down and landed on his nose. It woke him up. For a moment he remained quite still, blinking. Then suddenly he sat bolt upright and pushed his glasses higher on his nose.

He found his ink pen in the breast pocket of his overcoat. Tad's birthday book was in his lap, under the box of rubber bands. He turned to the last page and uncapped his pen. Then he wrote:

Chapter 8.

On a particular October afternoon,
Thaddeus Quimby Jones,
    also known as Tad, had a
birthday party outdoors....